There's a Yak in my Bed

Written by
K. Pluta

Illustrated by
Christy Stallop

Blooming Tree Press

To my sons, Bobby and Kip, who help me stay young and silly
- K.P.

For my two, Sam & Max
-C.S.

There's a Yak in my Bed

Blooming Tree Press
P.O. Box 140934
Austin, Texas 78714-0934
Copyright 2005 by K. Pluta
Cover art and interior illustrations by Christy Stallop
Book Design by Regan Johnson
Logo by Tabi Designs
Editor Madeline Smoot
ISBN: 0-9769417-4-0
www.bloomingtreepress.com

All rights reserved. No part of this book may be reproduced in any manner whatsoever without written permission. For information write to:

Blooming Tree Press
P.O. Box 140934
Austin, Texas 78714-0934

Library of Congress Cataloging-in-Publication Data

Pluta, K.
   There's a yak in my bed / by K. Pluta ; illustrated by Christy Stallop.
     p. cm.
   Summary: Ted wants to get rid of the yak he found in his bed, but first he must find out what it wants and how he can help.
   ISBN 0-9769417-4-0 (hardcover)
   [1. Yak--Fiction. 2. Humorous stories.]   I. Stallop, Christy, ill. II. Title.
PZ7.P738The 2007
[E]--dc22

2006022509

"**Mom!**" yelled Ted. "THERE'S A **YAK** IN MY BED!"

"Tell him to get out," said Mom. "It's time for breakfast."

"Get out of my bed," said Ted to the Yak.

"No," said the Yak. "Your bed is too soft."

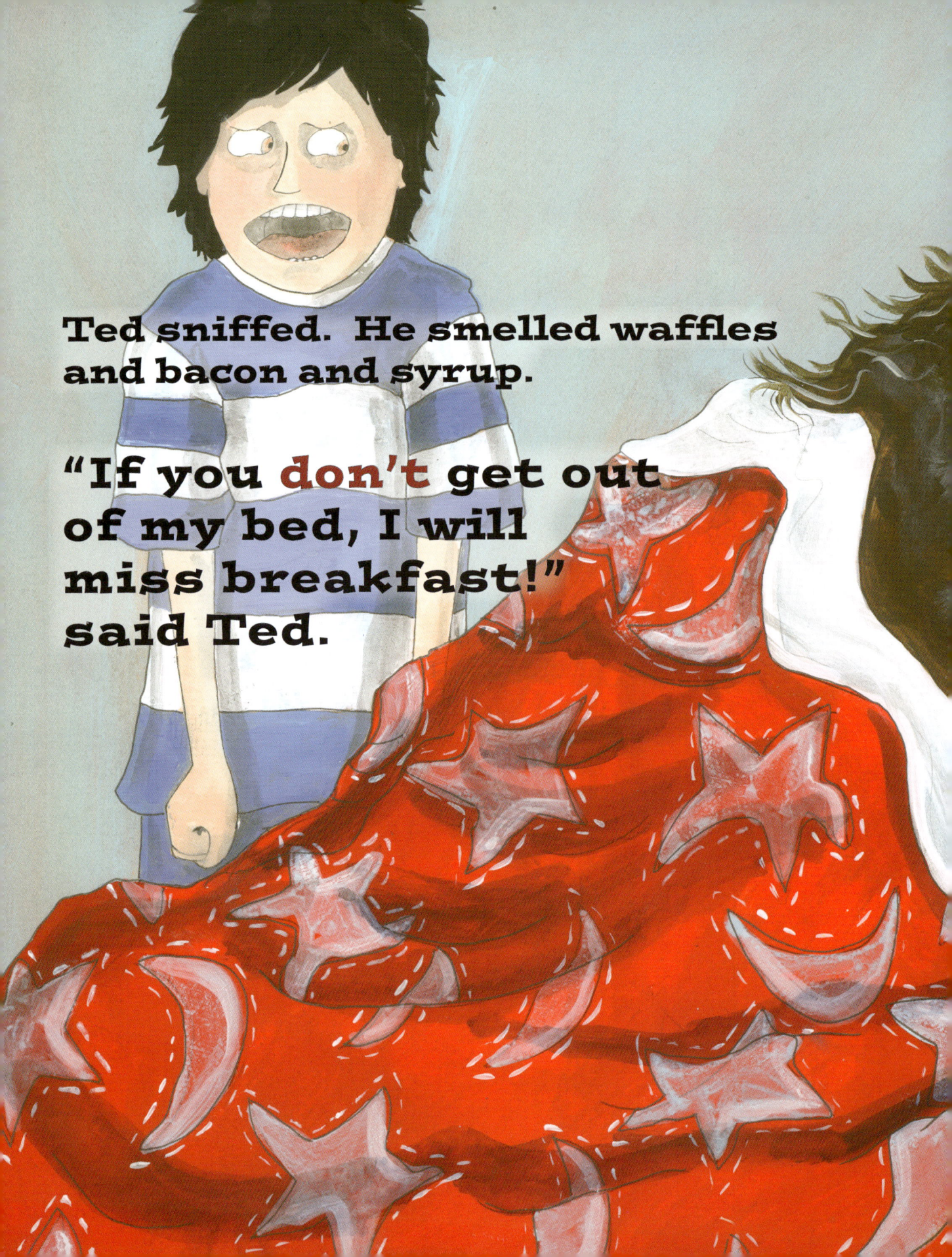

"There is no fox here," said Ted

"He might come by," said the Yak.

"I don't think so," said Ted.

"I've always heard you find things in the last place you look. I will stay here until I find Fox."

"I met him at a party. He said to **Keep in touch.**"

"**No**," said the Yak.

"**Why not?**" asked Ted.

"**Because** I have to tell **Fox** a secret," said the Yak. "If you write it, it won't be a secret anymore."

"**Then** you will have to go to **school** with me to learn to write," said Ted.

The Yak put on pants, and a shirt, and socks and shoes.

He hurried downstairs after Ted.

Mom was not wearing her glasses. She looked very tired. She gave Ted extra waffles. Ted shared. The Yak **burped.**

"Oh dear," said Mom to Ted. "You sound funny. Do you have a frog in your throat?"

"No," said Ted. "No frog in my throat. I did have a Yak in my bed. He's out now."

"Good," said Mom. She leaned over to kiss Ted on the head. She missed. "You need a haircut," she said.

Ted and the Yak sat across from Katie Jo Perkins.
"Good," said Ted. "I got you out of bed. We are on our way to school. You will learn to write. You will find Fox. Now, everything will be fine."